HAWKEYE™

MARK GRUENWALD
writer/penciler

BRETT BREEDING
DANNY BULANADI
inker/embellishers

BOB SHAREN
CHRISTIE SCHEELE
colorists

JOE ROSEN
letterer

DENNIS O'NEIL
series editor

GREGORY WRIGHT
trade paperback editor

TOM DeFALCO
editor in chief

MARK GRUENWALD
BRETT BREEDING
cover artists

HAWKEYE (including all prominent characters fea-
tured in this series), and the distinctive likenesses
thereof, are trademarks of the Marvel Entertainment
Group, Inc.

Published by Marvel Comics, a New World Pictures
Company, 387 Park Avenue South, New York, New
York, 10016.

ISBN 0-87135-364-4

FOREWORD

Since the dawn of the English language, there have been few legendary heroes who have had a greater hold on the collective imagination of our culture than Robin Hood. The rogue archer has spawned a host of literary heirs, particularly within the hybrid medium of the comic book. In the September 1964 issue of *Tales of Suspense*, Stan Lee and Don Heck gave us the Marvel Comics version of the archetypal archer. Hawkeye the Marksman began his career as an opponent of one of Marvel's premier super heroes, the invincible Iron Man. Inspired by the armored Avenger, Hawkeye wanted to be a hero, but a few run-ins with the law and association with the Russian spy, code-named Black Widow, got him branded a criminal. In his fourth appearance, however, he broke into the headquarters of the world's mightiest group of champions, the Avengers, and petitioned them for membership. Apparently impressed with his audacity and earnestness, the Avengers granted him membership, and for the next bunch of years, he proved himself in battle time and time again, relying entirely on his natural skills and prowess to keep pace with his superhumanly powered peers. (Okay, so for a brief time, Hawk did chuck in his bow to take a growth-gas so he could become a super-giant Goliath — nobody's perfect!)

Hawkeye's appeal goes beyond the raw charm of his basic, easy to understand weapon, the bow-and-arrow. It was his various character traits that catapulted him beyond the heroic archetype of Robin Hood from which he was derived. First there was his unflagging determination to go head-to-head with folks far more powerful than he. Hawkeye was a hero a reader could really identify with. No god, no mutant, no android, no recipient of cosmic or radioactive or chemical powers, Hawkeye was just a guy who practiced and practiced at something until he became so good at it that he could hold his own in the company of gods, mutants, androids, and recipients of cosmic, radioactive, and chemical powers. Wow, a hero you could really become if you were willing to work at it. And then, there was his lovable fallibility. Never a master planner or a deep thinker, Hawkeye would frequently find himself far over his head in hot water and have to use every bit of his skill and wits to get himself out. Such a contrast from his mentor and sometime babysitter, Captain America, who was always the self-assured master of whatever situation he found himself in. Hawkeye was obnoxious, cracking jokes at inappropriate moments, openly disrespectful of authority, grousing all the time — a general nuisance to have around. But we all knew it was because of his own insecurity and feeling of unworthiness. Here was a poor orphan, playing the world's most dangerous game, with every single person he met outclassing him in some way. How would you act in that case?

Anyway, Hawkeye put in long stints as an Avenger, and proved to be one of the most popular of the second-string heroes who never head their own solo features. It took Hawk nineteen years to get his first shot as a headliner. In the mini-series mania of 1983, I proposed a Hawkeye Limited Series, and got the go-ahead. As a bone to throw me, then editor in chief Jim Shooter said I could draw the series as well as write it. (I guess he felt sorry for me since I had been thrown off all the regular series I had been writing just prior to this — it's a long story.) This was a big thrill to me. I had, some five years earlier, first tried to break into The Business as an artist, and when my samples proved (shall we say) inadequate to do the job, I switched my emphasis to writing, and broke in as an assistant editor with writerly aspirations. Writing over other people's art for five years had taught me a lot about storytelling and drawing so I was tickled to finally have a chance to try to put what I learned on paper. So, undaunted by the fact that I don't draw all that well, I plunged ahead and produced the four issues of *Hawkeye* that are repackaged in this volume. Drawing them taught me a lot of things, foremost among which is that it takes four times as long to tell a story when you have to draw it yourself.

My philosophy of the Limited Series is that it should not only depict the single most important adventure of a hero's life, it should also leave the character permanently transformed by the experience. That's what I tried to do here. In these pages, Hawk meets Mockingbird, a woman who turns his life around. Mockingbird is one of my own contributions to the Marvel mythos (with creative input by fellow writer Steven Grant). Originally intended as a *Spider-Woman* nemesis, Mock fit the bill as an ideal counterpart to the maladjusted marksman — athletic, brainy, and as sharp-tongued as Hawk himself. Hawk had always been unlucky in love, falling for one unattainable woman after another. I felt it was high time he had somebody hot for him. Mockingbird was a former spy, like the other great love of Hawkeye's life, and the idea of a PhD in biology falling for a carnival archer who barely finished high school has a bizarre appeal to me.

Hawkeye and Mockingbird have since gone on to become founding members of the West Coast Avengers, appearing in a magazine by that title every month, and just recently Hawkeye got a second regular berth as the front feature in every monthly issue of *Solo Avengers*. A regular series all his own seems to be just around the corner for the battling bowman, and what with the trick arrows that are Hawkeye's stock in trade, hitting something around the corner shouldn't be much of a problem at all.

—Mark Gruenwald
New York City
1-17-88

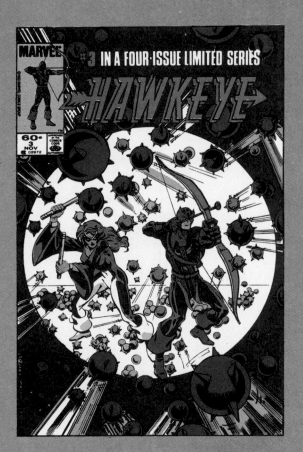

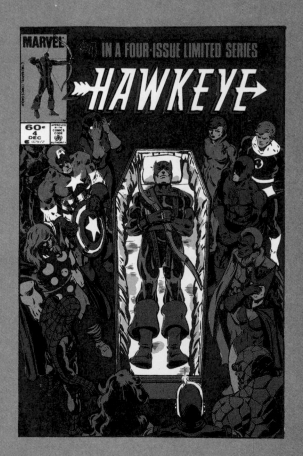

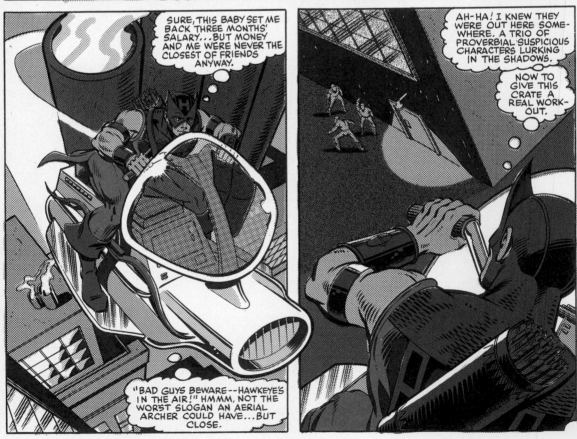

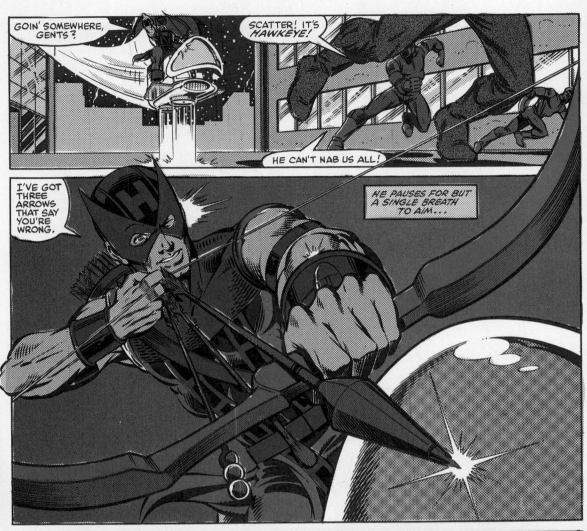

THREE SHOTS...

...THREE BULLSEYES.

I'LL JUST HAVE TO PUT THE 'SLED ON HOVER AND CHECK OUT MY ACCURACY UP-CLOSE AND IN PERSON.

THANKS A LOT, GUYS. I CAN JOYRIDE LIKE A TEENAGER WITH HIS FIRST SET OF WHEELS ALL I WANT, BUT UNLESS I CAN HANDLE THE 'SLED IN A COMBAT SITUATION, IT'S USE-LESS TO ME.

OUR PLEASURE, HAWK.

SPEAK FER YERSELF, LATHAM. YOU DIDN'T GET SHAFTED WITH A GLUE-ARROW! YER PAYIN' MY DRY-CLEANIN' BILLS, BOWMAN, Y'HEAR?

JORGIE BOY, YOU'RE A BLEEPING GENIUS. THE ROCKET-SLED HANDLES LIKE A REGULAR FLYING CARPET.

WELL, DESIGN-ING IT FOR YOUR RATHER UN-USUAL NEEDS WAS QUITE A TASK--

--BUT AT LEAST IT WAS A CHALLENGE COMPARED TO MOST OF THE DRUDGEWORK CROSS PAYS ME TO DO!

YOU REALLY OUGHTA GO INTO BUSINESS FOR YOUR-SELF, JORGE. YOU MIGHT EVEN GIVE TONY STARK A RUN FOR HIS MONEY.

SURE, HAWK, SUUUURE.

HEY, I WUZ MEANIN' TO ASK YA, HAWK, HOWCUM YA CARRY THAT ROBIN HOOD STUFF WHEN A .45 MAG-NUM IS A HUNNERT TIMES DEADLIER?

THE BOW IS QUIETER, MORE VERSATILE, AND IN MY HANDS THE DEADLIEST WEAPON IN THE STATE. OR HADN'T YOU NOTICED, HOWIE?

AH, LEMME SEE THAT THING. I USEDTA SHOOT A BOW 'N' ARROW --IN BOY SCOUTS --IT AIN'T SO HARD.

HERE.

UNNNNNGH.

PHOOEY. THERE'S GOTTA BE A TRICK TO IT.

YEP, THERE IS.

PRACTICE.

THERE YOU ARE, SHOWING OFF AGAIN.

GOOD EVENING, MISS DANNING.

HUH? HEY, SHEILA!

CHECK YOU LATER, JORGE. I'VE GOT SOME BUSINESS TO ATTEND TO. THANKS AGAIN.

I WAS JUST ABOUT TO HEAD UP TO YOUR OFFICE. WE STILL ON FOR TONIGHT?

YOU KNOW IT, CUPID.

C.T.E.'S SECURITY CHIEF DOESN'T HAVE THAT MANY NIGHTS OFF THAT I CAN AFFORD TO LET ONE GO BY.

NEITHER DOES C.T.E.'S SPANKING NEW PUBLIC RELATIONS LADY.

SO LET'S GET TO IT.

MILADY, YOUR CARRIAGE AWAITS.

HOLD TIGHT.

WITH YOU DRIVING, I WOULDN'T DREAM OF DOING OTHERWISE.

SAY, SINCE WHEN DOES THIS SNOWMOBILE FLY?

THE GUYS RIGGED UP THE ANTI-GRAV SYSTEM JUST TONIGHT. NEAT, HUH?

ROSS TECHNOLOGICAL ENTERPRISES

SOON, CROSSING THE EAST RIVER INTO MANHATTAN...

MAN, THIS IS THE LIFE! A RIDICULOUSLY HIGH-PAYING JOB, A FAST MACHINE BETWEEN MY LEGS, AND A FOXY LADY WHO'S NUTS ABOUT ME. WHAT MORE COULD A GUY WANT?

UNTIL SHEILA CAME ALONG, I THOUGHT I WAS PUT ON THIS WORLD FOR WOMEN TO DUMP ON.

WOMEN...LIKE THE BLACK WIDOW AND SCARLET WITCH. NO MATTER WHAT I DID, I JUST COULDN'T GET THEM TO CARE FOR ME LIKE I DID FOR THEM.

SHEILA'S DIFFERENT.

EVEN THOUGH WE'VE BEEN SEEING EACH OTHER FOR ONLY A MONTH, WHAT WE HAVE IS SPECIAL, REAL, LIKE NOTHING I'VE EVER KNOWN.

ATTENTION, PASSENGERS. THANK YOU FOR FLYING HAWK AIR. WE'LL BE ARRIVING AT CLINT BARTON'S BACHELOR PAD IN FIVE SECONDS.

GREAT MACHINE, ISN'T IT?

I MAY GET USED TO IT.

AFTER YOU, MADEMOISELLE...

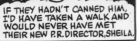

I'VE GOT NO SECRETS FROM YOU... LET'S SEE, MY MOM AND DAD DIED IN A CAR ACCIDENT WHEN I WAS A KID. MY BROTHER BARNEY AND I GOT STUCK IN AN ORPHANAGE.

"-- FOR A WHILE ANY-WAY. ONE NIGHT-- I WAS ABOUT 13 OR SO --BARNEY AND I RAN AWAY.

"WE WOUND UP AT THIS TRAVELING CARNIVAL THAT HAD JUST COME TO TOWN.

"WE TALKED TO A BUNCH OF CARNY FOLK, TRYING TO SCROUNGE UP A MEAL, A PLACE TO STAY...

"THEN I MET A GUY WHO WOULD CHANGE MY LIFE FOREVER -- THE STAR OF THE CARNIVAL, A JOE KNOWN AS THE SWORDSMAN...

SO YOU WANT TO WORK, EH, BOYS?

I MIGHT BE LOOKING FOR SOMEONE TO ASSIST ME IN MY ACT. I CAN ONLY USE ONE OF YOU, THOUGH.

"HE CHOSE ME, SAYING BARNEY WAS TOO OLD TO TRAIN RIGHT. HE GAVE ME MY FIRST BOW AND PLUNKED ME DOWN IN FRONT OF A TARGET AND TOLD ME TO GET TO IT.

"I DID... EAGERLY. SEE, THE SWORDSMAN BECAME LIKE A FATHER TO ME. I WORSHIPPED HIM--

"-- BUT FEARED HIM A LITTLE, TOO.

DON'T EVER FORGET... WHICH ONE OF US IS THE MASTER!

THUK

"I PRACTICED ARCHERY FOR HOURS EVERY DAY, HOPING TO GET GOOD ENOUGH SO THE SWORDSMAN WOULD LIKE ME.

"IN A YEAR OR SO I WAS GOOD ENOUGH TO JOIN HIM IN THE SHOW AS A TRICK SHOOTER.

"I WAS HAVING THE TIME OF MY LIFE, UNTIL...

HEY... DID YOU HEAR ABOUT THE PAYMASTER BEING ROBBED, AND--

WHA--

12

"HE SAID IF I PROMISED TO BE QUIET, I COULD BE HIS PARTNER...

"INSTEAD, I RAN.

"HE CHASED ME INTO THE MAIN TENT AND UP TO THE HIGH WIRE. FOR SOME REASON, I THOUGHT HE WOULDN'T FOLLOW ME.

"HE DID. IT WAS ABSURD: A DUEL OF ARROW AGAINST SWORD WHILE DANCING ON A TIGHTROPE.

"I WAS SCARED, HURT, NOT REALLY WANTING TO HIT HIM. TOO BAD HE DIDN'T FEEL THE SAME WAY.

"GOOD OL' BARNEY HEARD MY MOANING AND FOUND ME.

CLINT!

"ONE SLICE OF THE SWORD AND IT WAS OVER. THE SWORDSMAN LEFT ME IN A BROKEN HEAP AND SKIPPED TOWN.

"HE GOT ME TO THE MEDICS JUST IN TIME. WHEN HE WAS SURE I'D BE OKAY, HE TOOK OFF, TOO. GUESS HE HAD ENOUGH OF CARNY LIFE.

"I DIDN'T HEAR FROM HIM FOR YEARS. HE'S DEAD NOW.

"EVENTUALLY MY BROKEN BONES MENDED AND I RE-JOINED THE CARNIVAL.

"THAT'S WHERE I MET THE NEXT PERSON WHO'D TURN MY LIFE AROUND... IRON MAN!

"SEEING HIM GO INTO ACTION, I JUST KNEW THAT'S WHAT I WANTED TO DO WITH MYSELF.

"SO I MODIFIED MY CARNY OUTFIT A BIT AND STRODE OFF NAIVELY INTO THE NIGHT TO BECOME A HERO.

"UNFORTUNATELY, ON MY FIRST TIME OUT, I WAS MISTAKEN FOR A CROOK--

"AND ENDED UP GOING UP AGAINST THE VERY GUY WHO INSPIRED ME-- IRON MAN!

"SHELLHEAD LATER LEARNED MY TRUE MOTIVES, THOUGH. HE EVEN SPONSORED ME FOR MEMBERSHIP IN THE AVENGERS.

IT WAS THEN I KNEW I HAD REALLY MADE SOMETHING OF MYSELF.

I'VE DONE MANY A STINT WITH MY AVENGING BUDDIES, BUT I THINK I'M FINALLY READY TO WING IT SOLO FOR GOOD.

MUCH AS I LIKE 'EM, THEY CRAMP MY STYLE A BIT TOO MUCH.

FASCINATING STORY, CLINT. LOOKS LIKE I'VE GOT A REAL SELF-MADE MAN.

HOW ABOUT IF I TRY TO UNMAKE YOU A LITTLE?

LADY, ALL THE AVENGING IN THE WORLD CAN'T TAKE THE PLACE OF ONE OF YOUR--

BNNNNT

SMEK

AW, NO-- NOT MY EMERGENCY BEEPER.

IT WOULDN'T HAVE RUNG UNLESS SOMETHING BAD WAS GOING DOWN. I HATE TO DO THIS, BUT I'LL FEEL TERRIBLE IF I IGNORE IT.

OH, ALL RIGHT.

HOLD THAT POSE, DOLLFACE, I'LL BE BACK IN TWO SHAKES OF A LAMB'S TAIL.

PROMISE!

14

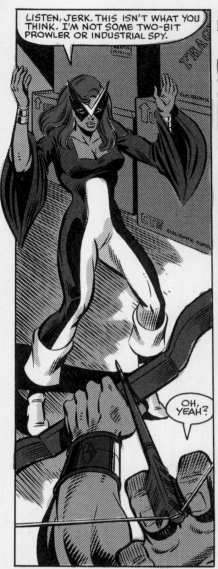

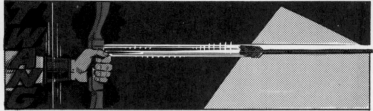

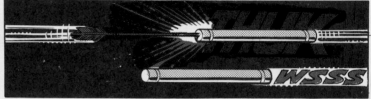

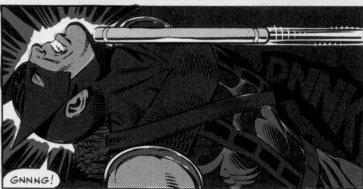

IF MY SOURCES PROVE TO BE WRONG, I'LL APOLOGIZE AND BE ON MY-- WHAT? THE *LIGHTS*--!

IT'S THE NIGHT SHIFT.

I THOUGHT I ORDERED THEM TO STAY PUT AND LET ME HANDLE THIS.

WE'LL TAKE HER, SIR.

HEY, MCDERMOTT! WHO'S IN CHARGE AROUND HERE? DIDN'T I SAY I'D SIGNAL YOU IF I NEEDED BACK-UP?

SIR, I THOUGHT YOU SENT THE SIGNAL. I--

AW, SKIP IT! YOU GUYS DID GOOD. NOW I CAN GET BACK TO MY NIGHT OFF.

MMMMFF?

TAKE GOOD CARE OF HER, GUYS. I'LL WANT TO QUESTION HER IN THE A.M.

I WONDER WHAT THAT MOCKINGBIRD CHICK WAS REALLY UP TO? COULD HER STORY BE STRAIGHT?

I'LL ADMIT I DON'T KNOW THE FULL SCOPE OF CTE'S MANUFACTUR-ING, AND THERE WAS THAT SHADY BUSINESS THAT EL AGUILA CLUED ME INTO.

I REALLY SHOULD CHECK IT ALL OUT. BUT FIRST I'D BETTER GET BACK TO A CERTAIN GORGEOUS LADY.

SOON, BACK AT HIS APARTMENT...

MAN, THIS LITTLE FIELD TRIP HAS GOTTEN ME WOUND UP. I'M NOT GOING TO BE ABLE TO GET BACK INTO THE SWING OF THE EVENING, I JUST KNOW IT.

SHEILA?

HI, BABE. I'M BACK.

OH, CLINT... I MUST'VE DOZED OFF. HOW'D IT GO? WHAT WAS THE PROBLEM?

JUST A SIMPLE BREAK-IN. THEY SHOULD HAVE BEEN ABLE TO HANDLE IT THEMSELVES. SOME OVERCAUTIOUS DESK JOCKEY DIDN'T WANT TO TAKE THE RESPONSIBILITY, I GUESS.

FORGET IT, HANDSOME. LET'S PICK UP WHERE WE LEFT OFF.

UH...

LISTEN, I KNOW THIS IS WEIRD, BUT SOMETHING'S BUGGING ME THAT I'VE GOT TO CHECK OUT.

AT CROSS?

YEAH. I'LL CALL A CAB AND DROP BY YOUR PLACE LATER.

I MUST HAVE A FEW SCREWS LOOSE TO LET BUSINESS MESS WITH MY PLEASURE ON MY NIGHT OFF. IT'S LIKE I WANT TO ROCK THE FIRST SMOOTH RELATIONSHIP I'VE EVER HAD.

OH, WELL, IF I CHECK OUT THIS WAREHOUSE 10, HAVE A FEW WORDS WITH MOCKINGBIRD... I'LL PUT MY MIND AT EASE.

IT'S STILL BEFORE MIDNIGHT. I CAN MAKE UP FOR LOST TIME WITH SHEILA LATER.

SOON...

HERE'S THE WAREHOUSE THE BIRD-LADY MENTIONED.

HMMM, I KNOW WHERE THE LIGHTBOX IS...

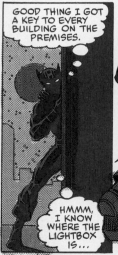

GOOD THING I GOT A KEY TO EVERY BUILDING ON THE PREMISES.

...BUT IF I SWITCH ON THE OVERHEADS, THE SECURITY ROOM WILL KNOW ABOUT IT. A FLARE ARROW WILL DO.

HMMM, THIS PLACE IS EMPTIER THAN MY WALLET THE DAY BEFORE PAYDAY. THE WAREHOUSE MUST NOW BE IN USE RIGHT NOW.

WAIT A MINUTE. FRESH TRACKS IN THE DUST. SOMETHING'S BEEN MOVED AROUND IN HERE...

...LIKE IN THE LAST HOUR OR SO! HEY, I THINK I HEAR--

--SOMETHING.

HI, FELLAS. WHAT'S HAPPENING?

HEY, HOLSTER THOSE POP-GUNS. I'M YOUR BOSS, REMEMBER? WANNA SEE MY I.D.?

THAT DON'T CUT IT NO MORE, HAWK.

NOW SET DOWN THAT BOW NICE AND EASY OR WE'LL COME AND TAKE IT FROM YA!

WELL, SINCE YOU ASKED SO POLITELY--

--GO STUFF YOURSELVES!

WHAT IN BLAZES IS WRONG WITH THESE JOKERS? I'LL HAVE THEIR JOBS FOR THIS!

I MUST BE NUTS TO THINK I'M GONNA OUTMATCH TWENTY HIGHLY-TRAINED, WELL-ARMED MEN--

--BUT I'LL BE HANGED IF I DON'T GIVE IT MY BEST SHOT!

HEY-- THAT SUCKER KILLED THE LIGHTS!

I KNOW WHERE HE ROLLED!

YAAAAH.

CHARLIE--?

BLAM

AAAAH!

THUNK

WHILE I LIE HERE QUIET AS A LIBRARY, ALL I HAVE TO DO IS AIM IN THE DIRECTION OF ANY NOISE.

I'M SURE TO TAKE DOWN SOMEBODY!

TWANG

AAAGHK!

THOOP

THERE'S STILL A FEW LEFT RUNNING AROUND, BUT I THINNED THEIR RANKS BUT GOOD.

NOW I'LL JUST BELLY TOWARDS WHERE I REMEMBER THE DOOR WAS AND HOPE NOBODY STEPS ON ME.

BUT-- COOL IT, HOTSHOT. I GOT A LADY HERE WHO'S GONNA GET DRILLED 'LESS YOU SURRENDER RIGHT NOW!

HAWK-- DO WHAT HE SAYS. IT'S SHEILA!

SHEILA-- HERE? BUT HOW? I THOUGHT SHE WAS HOME.

IT SOUNDED TOO MUCH LIKE HER TO RISK ANYTHING. I'D BETTER GIVE UP.

22

BARTON-- YOU STUPID FOOL! WHY DID YOU HAVE TO BE SO CONSCIENTIOUS? IT WAS MY JOB TO KEEP YOU DISTRACTED SO YOU'D HAVE NO TIME TO NOTICE THE OPERATION CROSS HAD BEEN CONTRACTED FOR--

--A VERY COSTLY, DEADLY OPERATION.

WHAT ARE YOU TALKING ABOUT, SHEILA? ARE YOU SAYING THEY PAID YOU TO-- TO--

YES, THEY PAID ME. I WAS PRETTY CONVINCING, WASN'T I? YOU NEVER HAD THE SLIGHTEST IDEA THAT I COULD SOONER LOVE A DOG THAN A CORNBALL ROMEO WITH DELUSIONS OF ADEQUACY LIKE YOU.

YOU CAN'T MEAN THAT! THEY MUST'VE BRAINWASHED YOU, POISONED YOUR MIND AGAINST ME! OR-- OR MAYBE YOU'RE NOT SHEILA AT ALL. AN IMPOSTOR, OR A ROBOT--!

DON'T KID YOURSELF, BARTON. I'M THE ONE AND ONLY. THE WOMAN WHO COULD BARELY KEEP FROM SNICKERING WHEN YOU TOLD HER YOUR CARNIVAL STORY THIS EVENING.

NOW YOU MUST EXCUSE ME. THE SANITATION CREW HAS ARRIVED AND I WOULDN'T WANT TO GET IN THE WAY OF THEIR WORK.

REPORT TO MY OFFICE WHEN THE JOB'S DONE, BOYS.

SLOOSH

UH-OH. WHAT'S THAT?

NOOO...

GAAAK. LIQUID INDUSTRIAL WASTE. WE'RE IN A STORAGE TANK FOR TOXIC SLUDGE!

HAWKEYE--?

23

IT-IT'S *HAWKEYE!* GET HIM! *GET HIM--!*

THOOM

THIS IS JUST BETWEEN YOU AND ME, BABE.

YOU HURT ME, SHEILA... MORE THAN ANYTHING EVER HURT IN MY LIFE.

STAY BACK, HAWKEYE! I-I--

I COULD KILL YOU FOR WHAT YOU DID TO ME.

BUT I WON'T. I... CAN'T. I JUST DON'T CARE ANY-MORE... ABOUT YOU OR ABOUT WHATEVER SCHEME CROSS IS UP TO!

GIVE ME MY BOW AND QUIVER BACK AND I'LL GO.

TAKE IT.

LISTEN, BARTON-- YOU KNOW TOO MUCH FOR US TO LET YOU WALK AWAY.

WE'RE GOING TO COME AFTER YOU. NO MATTER WHERE YOU RUN, WE'LL FIND YOU, I PROMISE YOU THAT. YOU HEAR?

27

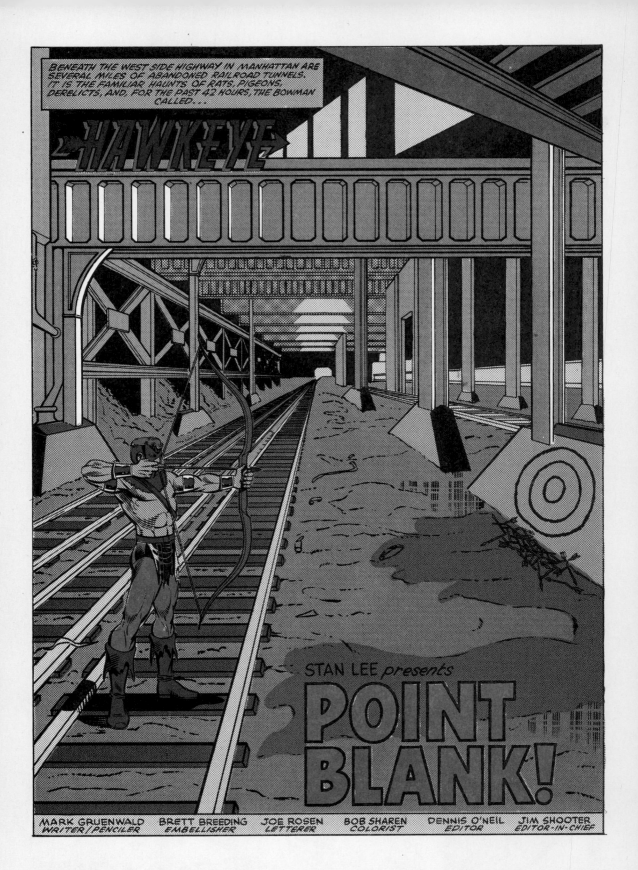

BENEATH THE WEST SIDE HIGHWAY IN MANHATTAN ARE SEVERAL MILES OF ABANDONED RAILROAD TUNNELS. IT IS THE FAMILIAR HAUNTS OF RATS, PIGEONS, DERELICTS, AND, FOR THE PAST 42 HOURS, THE BOWMAN CALLED...

HAWKEYE

STAN LEE *presents*

POINT BLANK!

MARK GRUENWALD	BRETT BREEDING	JOE ROSEN	BOB SHAREN	DENNIS O'NEIL	JIM SHOOTER
WRITER/PENCILER	EMBELLISHER	LETTERER	COLORIST	EDITOR	EDITOR-IN-CHIEF

REACH, NOTCH, DRAW, AIM...

....RELEASE.

HOW MANY TIMES HAS HE PERFORMED THIS FLUID SEQUENCE OF MOTIONS IN HIS LIFE? HOW MANY TIMES IN THE LAST 42 HOURS?

WHEN HIS QUIVER IS EMPTY, HE GOES TO THE TARGET AND RETRIEVES ANY ARROWS THAT CAN BE SHOT AGAIN.

WHOO

THERE ARE NOW ONLY SEVEN.

KTUNK

SIX.

KRNP

TA

HE HAS SHOT AT HIS MAKESHIFT CEMENT TARGET CONSTANTLY SINCE HE CAME HERE.

HE HAS YET TO HIT A BULLSEYE.

HE HAS BEEN CALLED THE WORLD'S GREATEST ARCHER. THAT DOESN'T MATTER NOW.

NOTHING MATTERS SINCE HE LOST HIS JOB, HIS HOME, AND THE WOMAN HE LOVED...ALL AT THE SAME MOMENT.

SO HE CAME HERE...AND AS THE HOURS PASSED, HIS RAGE TURNED TO NUMBNESS.

WITHOUT EATING, WITHOUT SLEEPING, WITHOUT HITTING A BULLSEYE, HE HAS SPENT THE PAST 42 HOURS ALONE...HERE.

HOW COULD IT HAVE HAPPENED? THROUGH THE FOG OF EXHAUSTION FRAGMENTS OF MEMORY APPEAR.

THERE WAS A BREAK-IN AT THE FACTORY WHERE HE WORKED SECURITY.

IT WAS A WOMAN, MOCKINGBIRD. SHE CLAIMED THERE WAS SOMETHING ILLEGAL AND DANGEROUS GOING ON AT THE PLANT.

THEN HIS OWN MEN TURNED AGAINST HIM...LEFT HIM IN A WASTE DISPOSAL UNIT TO DIE.

HE CALLED FOR SHIELA, THE WOMAN OF HIS HEART. SHE TOLD HIM SHE WAS IN ON IT.

SHE HAD BEEN HIRED TO ROMANCE HIM, ALLAY HIS SUS- PICIONS FROM THE ILLEGAL PROJECT CROSS TECH WAS ENGAGED IN.

LEARNING THAT, HE WANTED TO LIE BACK AND DIE. BUT SOMETHING PUSHED HIM TO GO ON...TO STRIKE BACK.

HE ESCAPED, BUT COULD NOT FIND A WAY TO VENT THE RAGE HE FELT.

FINALLY, FATIGUE OVERTAKES HIM.

KRMPH

TIME PASSES. THEN...

HEY HEY HEY, WHAT HAVE WE HERE?

SOME STIFF THINKS HE'S ROBIN HOOD.

THAT'S ONE 'A THEM COSTUMED DO-GOODER ZOIDS.

YEAH... NIGHTHAWK I THINK'S HIS NAME.

HE DEAD?

NAW, DRUNK OR O.D.ED ON SOMETHING. STILL BREATHING.

THESE SUPER-DOOPS DON'T LOOK SO TOUGH UP CLOSE, HUH?

WHAT SAY WE PUT THIS ONE OUTTA HIS MISERY?

HEY, FORGET HIM. LOOK AT THIS! SOME KINDA SUPER-CYCLE WIDDOUT WHEELS!

LATER, MUD!

I HATE THESE DO-GOODER TYPES. ONE OF 'EM PUT MY OL' MAN IN THE JOINT. LET'S CUT 'IM UP...BAD.

FLIK

MINUTES LATER, AT CENTRAL PARK WEST AND 80TH...

THIS COULD BE A TRAP.

CROSS COULD HAVE THIS PLACE STAKED OUT, JUST WAITING FOR ME.

I DON'T SEE ANYONE.

WHEW. DID THEY EVER CLEAN THIS PLACE OUT. EVERYTHING I OWNED... GONE.

MY ARROW-MAKING TOOLS...

MY VIDEO RECORDER...

MY ROCK'N'ROLL RECORDS...

MY SPARE COSTUMES...GONE.

BLAST.

BEST PLACE I EVER LIVED IN.

WELL, IT'S BACK TO SKID ROW FOR CLINTON F. BARTON, ARROW-CHUCKER AND NOBODY'S SWEETHEART.

HELLO, HAWK. CAN I BUY YOU SOME BREAKFAST?

MOCKINGBIRD!

FAIR ENOUGH. LET'S SEE... MY REAL NAME'S *BARBARA MORSE*. FRIENDS CALL ME BOBBI.

"I WAS YOUR TYPICAL A-PLUS STUDENT AT GEORGIA TECH. WHEN MY FAVORITE PROF. DR. WILMA CALVIN, TOOK A SABBATICAL TO WORK ON A GOVERNMENT PROJECT, I SIGNED ON WITH HER.

"TURNED OUT THE PROJECT WAS RECOVERING THE SUPER-SOLDIER FORMULA THAT MADE CAPTAIN AMERICA WHAT HE IS.

"SINCE S.H.I.E.L.D. WAS ONE OF THE MAJOR SPONSORS OF THE PROJECT, I GOT TO KNOW A FEW AGENTS.

"THOUGH I LIKED BIOLOGY, I LOVED THE IDEA OF BECOMING MATA HARI. SO I ENROLLED IN S.H.I.E.L.D.'S SPY SCHOOL.

"I GRADUATED AT THE TOP OF THE CLASS, THEN I WAS GIVEN MY FIRST FIELD MISSION: TO TRACK DOWN A CERTAIN WILD MAN BY THE NAME OF *KA-ZAR*, WHOSE JUNGLE SKILLS S.H.I.E.L.D. WANTED TO EMPLOY...

"I FOUND THE JUNGLE MAN ALL RIGHT, EVEN GOT INVOLVED WITH HIM, IF YOU KNOW WHAT I MEAN.

"BUT THINGS NEVER QUITE WORKED OUT BETWEEN US.

"I WAS A FIELD AGENT FOR S.H.I.E.L.D. FOR A BIT, THEN AT THE REQUEST OF A CONGRESSMAN, I DID A COVERT OPERATION INSIDE S.H.I.E.L.D. ITSELF, TRYING TO SNIFF OUT CORRUPTION.

"I CALLED MYSELF THE *HUNTRESS*, AND THANKS TO PARTIES UNDER SUSPICION, I GAINED A REPUTATION AS A TRAITOR TO THE ORGANIZATION.

"I CHANGED MY CODE NAME TO *MOCKINGBIRD* AND TOOK MY EVIDENCE OF AGENTS NOT ON THE UP-AND-UP TO HEAD HONCHO *NICK FURY*.

"UNFORTUNATELY I TOOK A FEW BULLETS, TOO, FROM A FEW OVERZEALOUS S.H.I.E.L.D. AGENTS.

"I SPENT THE NEXT SIX MONTHS IN A PRIVATE HOSPITAL CONVALESCING.

"WHEN I RECOVERED, I TURNED DOWN A S.H.I.E.L.D. PROMOTION TO GO SOLO.

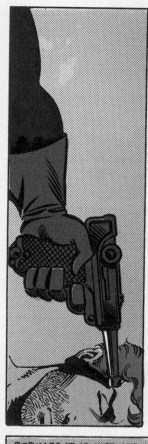

PERHAPS IT IS INSTINCT-- A SURVIVAL SENSE HONED IN HUNDREDS OF LIFE-AND-DEATH STRUGGLES...

BUT SOMEHOW CLINT BARTON FEELS THE COOL GUN METAL AT HIS TEMPLE, INSTANTLY RECOGNIZES IT FOR WHAT IT IS--

--AND REACTS.

HOO-EEE! WHAT THE HEY IS GOING ON? ONE MINUTE MOCK IS TELLING ME A BEDTIME STORY, THE NEXT I'M SOME YAHOO'S TARGET PRACTICE.

I'VE GOT TO GET TO MY BOW 'N' ARROWS BEFORE I'M SMOKED MEAT!

IT FIGURES. I LEFT 'EM ON THE OTHER SIDE OF THE ROOM. I'LL NEED COVER TO GET THERE.

THIS'LL DO. HEY, I JUST NOTICED SOMETHING. MR. SHARPSHOOTER'S GUN DOESN'T MAKE A SOUND WHEN IT FIRES -- NOT THE SLIGHTEST SOUND.

NEITHER DO THE BULLETS WHEN THEY HIT. WHAT KIND OF SILENCER DOES THIS GUY USE?

I'LL WORRY ABOUT THAT LATER. FIRST I GOTTA ROLL THIS TABLE TOWARDS MY BOW AND HOPE THAT SILENT SAM DOESN'T CATCH ON TO WHAT I'M--

--DOING.

OH, NO!

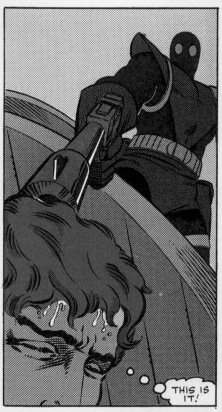

THIS IS IT!

WHAT THE?

LOOKS LIKE I GOT BACK JUST IN THE NICK.

HAWK-- GRAB HIS GUN!

42

WHAT HAPPENED TO YOU, MAN? WE GOT A MEMO TWO DAYS AGO THAT YOU WERE FIRED FOR INCOMPETENCY, AND I HAVEN'T SEEN YOU SINCE!

IT'S A LONG STORY, JORGE.

THIS IS MY ASSOCIATE, MOCKING-BIRD. MOCK, THIS IS *JORGE LATHAM*, THE GUY WHO DESIGNED MY SKY-MOBILE AND THE ONLY GUY AT CROSS I CAN TRUST.

HI.

COME ON IN. I'LL GRAB US SOME BREW.

I GOT TO TELL YOU, HAWK, YOU ARE DEFINITELY PERSONA NON GRATA AROUND THE PLANT. THEY'RE OFFERING A YEAR'S SALARY TO ANYONE WHO SEES YOU ANYWHERE ON THE GROUNDS. WHAT'S GOING ON?

SOMETHING IS REALLY ROTTEN AT CROSS. SOMEBODY HIGH IN MANAGE-MENT IS INVOLVED IN SOME KIND OF PROJECT--WE'RE NOT YET SURE EXACTLY WHAT--THAT'S GOING TO ENDANGER A LOT OF LIVES. THEY THOUGHT I KNEW TOO MUCH ABOUT IT--AND FIRED ME.

YOU WOULDN'T HAPPEN TO BE WORKING ON ANYTHING FUNNY IN THE DESIGN DEPART-MENT, WOULD YOU, JORGE?

JUST THE USUAL, BORING STUFF. ALL THE SPECIAL PROJECTS ARE DONE BY THE BRAIN-BOYS ON THE 17TH FLOOR.

AFTER BEING BRIEFED ABOUT THE CHANGES IN CROSS SECURITY...

LISTEN, JORGE, IF I WERE YOU, I'D START PREPARING A RESUME. IF THIS IS AS BIG AS I THINK, WE'RE GOING TO SHUT CROSS DOWN.

THANKS FOR THE TIP, HAWK.

TAKE CARE! NICE MEETING YOU, MOCKINGBIRD!

THE INFO HE GAVE US IS GOING TO SAVE US A LOT OF HASSLE. SURE IS GOOD TO HAVE A FEW FOLKS YOU CAN TRUST.

YOU STILL DON'T QUITE TRUST *ME*, DO YOU, HAWKEYE? EVEN AFTER I SAVED YOUR LIFE.

NO OFFENSE, LADY, BUT IT'S GOING TO TAKE ME A WHILE BEFORE I CAN FULLY TRUST *ANY* WOMAN AGAIN.

AND... HERE WE ARE... ONE OF THE LAST PLACES IN THE WORLD I FEEL LIKE VISITING AGAIN.

CROSS TECHNOLOGICAL

THIS IS THE ADMINISTRATION AND ENGINEERING BUILDING. IF RECORDS OF PROJECT X ARE ANYWHERE, THEY'LL BE HERE.

AND UNLESS I'VE FORGOTTEN EVERYTHING I LEARNED IN A YEAR OF NIGHTLY ROUNDS--

--THIS IS THE SPECIAL DESIGNS DEPARTMENT.

THE ELECTRONIC SECURITY SYSTEM ON THE WINDOWS IS QUITE SOPHISTICATED...

...BUT I'VE GOT A FEW GIMMICK ARROWHEADS IN MY TUNIC POUCHES--

--THAT'LL SHORT CIRCUIT THIS SYSTEM IN A JIF. THIS NEUTRALIZER GIZMO WAS DESIGNED BY CROSS'S GREATEST RIVAL, I'M PROUD TO SAY-- TONY STARK.

AND AFTER JIMMYING OPEN THE WINDOW WITH EQUAL EASE...

TA-DAA! INSIDE WITHOUT A HITCH.

WE'D BETTER WORK IN THE DARK SO NO ONE SEES THE LIGHT GO ON.

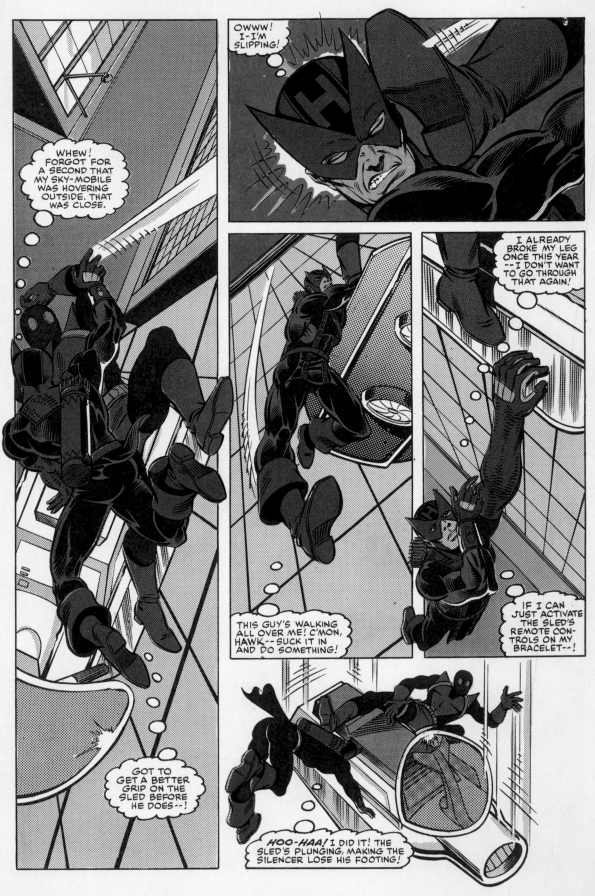

48

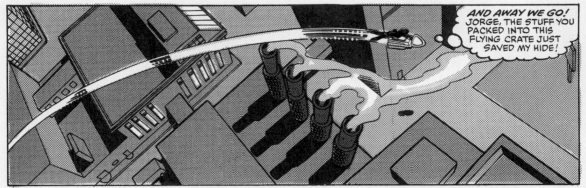

AND AWAY WE GO! JORGE, THE STUFF YOU PACKED INTO THIS FLYING CRATE JUST SAVED MY HIDE!

WHOOP. KIND OF HARD TO STEER AND FIGHT AT THE SAME TIME!

AW, NOT AGAIN! I'M SLIDING OFF--!

HE- HE LOST HIS GRIP, TOO!

MISSED THE EDGE--!

THE SILENT ASSASSIN SEEMS TO LISTEN FOR THE THUD OF HIS FOE'S BODY AS IT HITS THE BOTTOM OF THE SMOKESTACK--

BUT THE SOUND IS MUFFLED-- SWALLOWED IN THE IMPENETRABLE DARKNESS AT HIS FEET.

THE SILENCER TURNS, LOOKING FOR THE EASIEST WAY DOWN FROM HIS 200-FOOT HIGH PERCH.

HE SOON FINDS IT.

OH, MAN--I MUST'VE GIVEN MYSELF HEAD-TO-TOE BRUISES, BUT IF IT WEREN'T FOR THESE TWO HANDY SUCTION-CUP ARROWHEADS, I MIGHT'VE GIVEN MYSELF A HEAD TO TOE SPLAT!

I HOPE SILENCER HAS AS MUCH FUN AS I DID.

AFTER SUMMONING HIS SKY-SLED...

WONDER HOW MOCKINGBIRD IS DOING. WE MUST HAVE TRIPPED SOME KIND OF ALARM IF SILENCER KNEW WHERE TO FIND US.

NO TELLING WHO ELSE MIGHT HAVE BEEN SENT.

HAWK! THERE YOU ARE. I WAS BEGINNING TO WORRY.

NO NEED. I'M A BIG BOY.

DID YOU GET THE INFORMATION?

YOU BETCHA. THE BLUE-PRINTS, THE CLIENT'S NAME AND ADDRESS ...EVERYTHING.

RUN INTO ANY TROUBLE?

"NOT REALLY."

NEXT

BEHIND THE 8-BALL!

"THEY'RE GOING IN THE ROOF ENTRANCE..."

"...DOWN THE STAIRS..."

"RIGHT ABOUT NOW THEY SHOULD BE AT THE DOOR TO MOCKINGBIRD'S APARTMENT.

"SHE PUTS HER KEY IN THE DOOR, OPENS IT.

"THEY STEP IN. THE DOOR SHUTS. NOW!"

BAROOM

BLOOEY!

SEEN ONE BURNING BUILDING, YOU SEEN THEM ALL. C'MON, DOLLFACE. YOUR WAY MAY HAVE BEEN QUICKEST, BUT MINE'LL BE A LOT MORE FUN. LET'S GET TO SOMEWHERE WE CAN KEEP TABS ON THEM.

THEY WERE LUCKY THIS TIME. NEXT TIME THEY WON'T BE.

IT IS FIVE MINUTES BEFORE THE NEW YORK FIRE DEPARTMENT ARRIVES... TWO HOURS BEFORE THE BLAZE IS UNDER CONTROL.

FOR THOSE TWO HOURS, MOCKINGBIRD WATCHES IN INCREASINGLY SULLEN FASCINATION AS HER BELONGINGS AND HOME ARE CONSUMED BY SMOKE AND FLAME. THEN...

UH, LISTEN, MOCK. IT'LL BE HOURS BEFORE THIS PLACE IS COOL ENOUGH TO CHECK THE DAMAGE UP CLOSE.

SO WHY DON'T WE TAKE A WALK, GRAB SOMETHING TO EAT?

ALL RIGHT.

HMMM, SHE'S KINDA UPSET ABOUT THIS, I THINK.

54

THAT EVENING...

SHEESH, WHAT A MESS.

I HAVE YET TO FIND A SINGLE THING I OWN IN ONE PIECE. VERY THOROUGH AND PROFESSIONAL JOB.

AND HERE'S WHAT'S LEFT OF MY PRIZE POSSESSION, MY BRAND NEW HIGH-FLYING SKY-MOBILE.

I HARDLY HAD A CHANCE TO ENJOY IT.

GEE WHIZ.

YOU GOT YOUR APARTMENT TAKEN AWAY, I GOT MINE BLOWN UP. LOOKS LIKE ALL WE HAVE LEFT IS--

--EACH OTHER.

UH, I DOUBT WE'RE GOING TO LEARN MUCH FROM SIFTING THROUGH THE RUBBLE. LET'S GO.

WHAT A DUNCE I AM. HE WAS JUST BEGINNING TO RELAX AROUND ME.

NOW I GO AND SPOOK HIM BY THROWING MYSELF UPON HIM. NNNH!

HEY, WHAT'S THIS?

WHAT'S WHAT?

WELL, AT LEAST SOMETHING OF YOURS SURVIVED.

ONLY THING IS-- I DON'T OWN AN 8-BALL.

HMMMM.

THE WAY I HAVE IT FIGURED, CROSS TECH* MUST HAVE LEARNED WE STOLE THE SHIPPING ORDER FOR THEIR DEATH DEVICE...

...SO THEY SENT OUT SOME MORE HIT MEN TO TRY TO SNUFF US.

THAT'S MY GUESS, TOO, SHERLOCK. LOOKS LIKE WE'D BETTER GET TO WHOEVER'S BEHIND THIS BEFORE HE OR SHE GETS TO US.

* THE MANUFACTURING OUTFIT WHICH USED TO EMPLOY HAWKEYE AS SECURITY CHIEF.

HOW YOU FIXED FOR CASH?

THAT MEAL I TREATED YOU TO WIPED ME OUT. FORTUNATELY, MY BANK'S ONLY A FEW BLOCKS FROM HERE. COME ON.

METROBANK 24 HOUR BAN

NOW, BY THE WONDERS OF AUTOMATION, I'LL WITHDRAW WHAT WE NEED.

WHAT? ONLY 97 DOLLARS IN MY ACCOUNT? MY LAST DEPOSIT MUST NOT HAVE CLEARED.

Here is
You hav
$97.00 o
$97.00 availa
May I help y
somethin

BETTER TAKE IT ALL, MOCK. WE'RE GOING TO NEED IT.

IF YOU SAY SO.

AND...

NOW WHAT IS IT YOU NEED ALL THIS CASH FOR?

IN CASE YOU HAVEN'T NOTICED, BIRDIE, I'M DOWN TO MY LAST ARROW. GOT TO BUY MORE.

I THOUGHT YOU NEEDED SPECIALLY MADE ARROWS.

MY NEW MODULAR ARROWHEADS FIT ON ANY TARGET ARROW... GET 'EM AT ANY SPORTING-GOODS STORE.

WITHIN THE HOUR...

HAPPY NOW?

YOU BETCHA.

SPORTING GOODS

GOSH, I LOVE ARROWS.

NOW LET'S GET THIS SHOW UNDERWAY. OKAY, MR. EYE?

TAXI!

HUH?

SPORT GOOD

LISTEN, BIRDBRAIN, WE CAN'T AFFORD A CAB TO THE UPPER EAST SIDE WITH WHAT WE HAVE LEFT.

Subway 4 5 6

WE'VE GOT TO SUB IT.

TWO PLEASE.

SINCE GETTING THOSE ARROWS, HAWKEYE'S DISPOSITION CERTAINLY HAS IMPROVED.

SO AFTER WE GET TO THE ADDRESS ON THE SHIPPING LIST, WE STAKE OUT THE PLACE UNTIL THE WEE HOURS OF THE MORNING, THEN SNEAK IN AND HAVE A LOOK AROUND.

YOU REALLY THINK THEY'RE NOT EXPECTING US?

SURE THEY'RE EXPECTING US. BARGING INTO LIONS' DENS IS ONE OF MY SPECIALTIES.

HOW ABOUT BARGING OUT OF THEM?

I'M STILL WORKING ON THAT.

YOU KNOW, THANKS TO OUR MONETARY LIMITATIONS, WE'RE PRETTY VISIBLE TARGETS FOR ANY CROSS HITMAN THAT COMES ALONG.

ON THE OTHER HAND, WHAT SELF-RESPECTING HITMAN WOULD TRY TO PULL OFF A JOB WITH SO MANY WITNESSES AROUND?

HIDING IN PLAIN SIGHT, HUH?

GOING TO A COSTUME PARTY, PAL?

NOW THIS I DON'T NEED, SOME BIG BOHUNK LOOKING TO IMPRESS HIS GIRL BY HASSLING THE BIG BAD SUPER HERO.

WAIT, IT'S *CAPTAIN AMERICA* IN HIS CIVVIES!

STEVE!

HOW YOU DOING, HAWKEYE? I HAVEN'T SEEN YOU IN WEEKS.

YEAH, WELL, UH, I'VE BEEN BUSY WITH THIS AND THAT. THE USUAL.

I TAKE IT FROM YOUR ATTIRE THAT YOU'RE ON A MISSION. IF YOU NEED HELP, I'D BE GLAD TO DROP WHAT I'M DOING AND PITCH IN.

AW, NO. CAP IS MR. AVENGERS HIMSELF. I KNOW I'M AT THE END OF MY RESOURCES, MAYBE WAY OUT OF MY DEPTH, BUT IF I LET CAP IN ON IT, HE'LL WIND UP RUNNING THE SHOW...

...AND I'LL END UP ON THE SIDELINES AGAIN, JUST LIKE IT WAS BACK IN THE AVENGERS.

AH, IT'S NOTHING I CAN'T HANDLE, OLD TIMER. JUST THE SAME OLD BOPPING THE BAD GUYS STUFF.

I READ YOU, SOLDIER.

ANYWAY, YOU KNOW HOW TO REACH ME IF YOU GET IN A JAM.

WELL, THIS IS WHERE I GET OFF. SEE YOU AROUND, PAL!

TAKE CARE!

GOD, IS HE GORGEOUS! HE'S ONE OF *US*, RIGHT?

YEP.

HOW COME YOU DIDN'T INTRODUCE HIM TO ME?

I FORGOT.

SHE MEETS CAP IN HIS CIVVIES AND IS BOWLED OVER. NO WONDER I ALWAYS LOOKED LIKE A PIKER AROUND HIM. YOU KNOW, I NEVER REALIZED HOW SECOND RATE CAP MAKES ME FEEL.

I'VE JUST GOT TO SOLVE THIS WHOLE MESS ON MY OWN. IF I DON'T, I MAY NEVER BE ABLE TO STAND ON MY OWN--

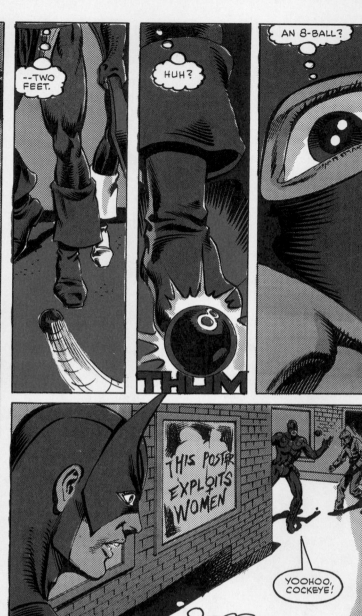

--TWO FEET.

HUH?

AN 8-BALL?

THUM

THIS POSTER EXPLOITS WOMEN

YOOHOO, COCKEYE!

WHO THE--?

I KNOW IT'S DUMB TO LET A PROBABLE HITMAN BAIT ME--

-- BUT I'M ITCHIN' FOR ACTION!

MOCK! I THINK WE'VE FOUND THE BOMBER!

HMMM. HE DIDN'T GET FAR. GUESS HE WANTS ME TO CATCH UP.

MY HEAVENS--!

DAG!

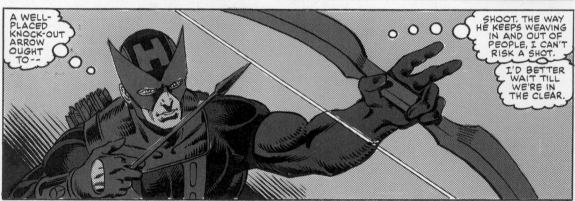

A WELL-PLACED KNOCK-OUT ARROW OUGHT TO--

SHOOT. THE WAY HE KEEPS WEAVING IN AND OUT OF PEOPLE, I CAN'T RISK A SHOT.

I'D BETTER WAIT TILL WE'RE IN THE CLEAR.

THERE'S GOT TO BE MORE TO THIS THAN MEETS THE EYE. WHAT KIND OF HITMAN WOULD LEAD US ON A WILD CHASE THROUGH GRAND CENTRAL STATION UNLESS HE HAD SOME KIND OF AMBUSH SET UP?

PARDON ME. COMING THROUGH.

ULLLLLHHHG!

BOOM

COME ON, CONDUCTOR. OPEN THE DOOR.

SO LONG, SUCKER!

SLAM

I HATE DITCHING MOCKINGBIRD, BUT I'M SURE SHE'LL HAVE THE BRAINS TO FIND ME.

CAN'T LET THIS ODDBALL CHARACTER GET AWAY.

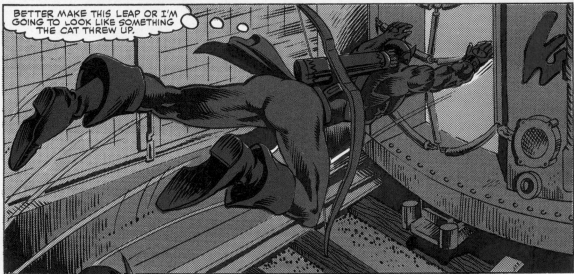

BETTER MAKE THIS LEAP OR I'M GOING TO LOOK LIKE SOMETHING THE CAT THREW UP.

DID IT!

MAN, THERE'S NOTHING LIKE A GOOD CHASE TO MAKE ME FEEL GREAT ABOUT MYSELF AGAIN. WONDER IF ODDBALL WOULD CONSENT TO BE MY REGULAR SPARRING PARTNER?

CAP'S GOT THE RED SKULL, IRON MAN HAS THE MANDARIN. ME, I NEVER HAD ANYBODY ALL MY OWN.

LUCK'S WITH ME. THE DOOR'S UNLOCKED.

IF IT CONCERNS YOU

HEY, ANYBODY SEE A GUY IN A COSTUME GO BY?

HE-HE WENT THAT WAY!

THREE CARS LATER...

STOP WHERE YOU ARE, ARROW FLYNN--

--OR THIS BYSTANDER GETS IT.

HEH-HEH. LOOK, EVERYBODY. THIS GUY'S GONNA JUGGLE ME TO DEATH!

WHAT--?

WISE GUY, HUH?

I HATE WISE GUYS.

ON SECOND THOUGHT, THIS GUY'S TOO SICK TO BE MY REGULAR FOE!

HOLD IT, SLEEZEBALL!

WHA--

AT LEAST I MANAGED TO CUT HIS AMMO IN HALF.

NOW, NOW, YOU WOULDN'T WANT TO WRECK CITY PROPERTY, WOULD YOU?

AND WHEN THE TRAIN STOPS AT TIMES SQUARE...

I'LL JUST SLIP OUT BETWEEN CARS BEFORE THEY OPEN THE DOORS.

EXIT

AND THE CHASE IS ON!

I COULD PICK HIM OFF ANY TIME I WANT. I KNOW I CAN THROW FASTER THAN HE CAN SHOOT.

BUT I'M HAVING JUST PLAIN TOO MUCH FUN TO CUT IT SHORT.

OH, HE FLEW THROUGH THE AIR WITH THE GREATEST FINESSE--

--THAT DARING YOUNG MAN ON HIS FLYING BUTTRESS!

WHEN IT COMES TO TRICKS, BABY--

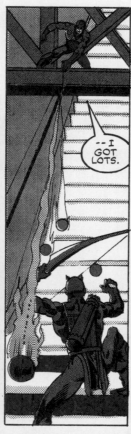

--I GOT LOTS.

I WANT TO TAKE YOU HIGHER, BOOMLACKA LACKA LACKA!

THIS GUY'S A LOON.

CAN'T GET A CLEAR SHOT FROM DOWN HERE.

THIS IS A BIT BETTER. REMINDS ME OF THE HIGHWIRE BACK IN MY CARNY DAYS.

OKAY, BALLZO, ENOUGH OF THIS HORSEPLAY. LET'S GET DOWN TO IT--MY ARROWS AGAINST YOUR UH, SPHERES.

TWANG

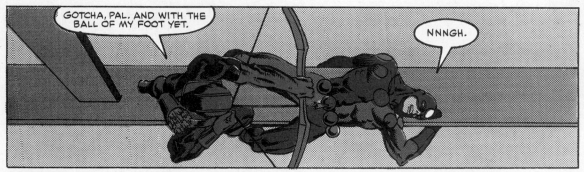

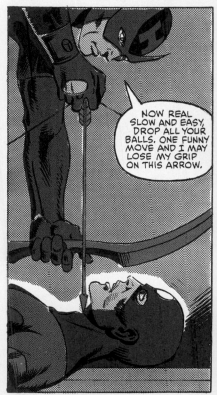

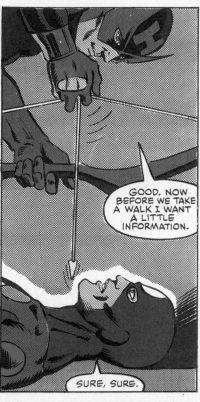

DON'T LOOK NOW, BUT I THINK WE'VE GOT COMPANY.

GOOD MORNING. I BELIEVE YOU HAVE ALREADY MET MY AGENTS, ODDBALL AND BOMBSHELL.

I AM *CROSSFIRE*-- MASTER SUBVERSIVE, BRAINWASHER, AND ENTREPRENEUR.

AS YOU MAY HAVE ALREADY SURMISED, I AM THE ONE WHO DISPATCHED ODDBALL AND BOMBSHELL AS WELL AS THE STILL-MISSING SILENCER TO DEAL WITH YOU.

I AM ALSO THE ONE, HAWKEYE, WHO CONTRACTED THE COMPANY YOU USED TO WORK FOR TO BUILD THE COMPONENTS TO PROJECT: UNDERTAKER. MORE ON THAT IN A MOMENT. FIRST, IN THE TYPICAL FASHION OF SOMEONE WHO HOLDS ALL THE CARDS, I'M GOING TO DIVULGE TO YOU MORE THAN YOU WILL NEED TO KNOW ABOUT ME AND MY BUSINESS...

"I AM A FORMER CENTRAL INTELLIGENCE AGENT. MY SPECIALTY--INFORMATION GATHERING AND EXTRACTING.

"WHEN MY INTERESTS VEERED SHARPLY FROM THOSE OF THE AGENCY, I QUIT AND USED MY RESOURCES AND CONTACTS TO ORGANIZE A PRIVATE ARMY OF MERCENARIES.

"MY MISSION IS TO FOMENT DISORDER FOR PROFIT.

"TO PREVENT FUTURE OPPOSITION, I HAVE UNDERTAKEN A PROGRAM TO ELIMINATE ALL COSTUMED SUPERHUMANS. BEFORE I WAS READY TO LAUNCH MY PLAN, HOWEVER, MOON KNIGHT AND THE THING INTERVENED...*

*MARVEL TWO-IN-ONE #52.

"ALTHOUGH THEY SUCCEEDED IN DESTROYING A PROTOTYPE OF MY UNDERTAKER WEAPON AND CORRALLED MY PRIVATE ARMY--

"-- I MANAGED TO ESCAPE, AND BEGAN MY WORK ANEW. YOU, HAWKEYE, PLAY A PIVOTAL ROLE IN MY GRAND PROJECT...

"AFTER I KILL YOU, WE'LL LEAVE YOUR BODY IN CENTRAL PARK WHERE IT IS BOUND TO BE DISCOVERED WITHIN A DAY.

"YOU WILL THEN BE TAKEN TO THE CITY MORGUE WHERE ONE OF YOUR AVENGER COMPATRIOTS WILL IDENTIFY AND CLAIM YOUR BODY.

"THE AVENGERS WILL THEN CALL ME TO ARRANGE YOUR FUNERAL. HOW DO I KNOW THIS? NOT ONLY IS THE RESTWELL FUNERAL PARLOR THE ESTABLISHMENT THAT YOUR ASSOCIATES USED THE LAST TIME ONE OF THEIR COMRADES-IN-ARMS PERISHED -- THE WHIZZER -- I HAVE ALSO ARRANGED THAT ALL THE OTHER MORTUARIES IN THE CITY ARE ENGAGED.

⊙ Restwell Funeral

"ENVISION IT, HAWKEYE, A PRIVATE MEMORIAL SERVICE FOR YOU IN MY SPECIALLY DESIGNED CHAPEL.

"THE RESULT WILL BE PANDEMONIUM AS YOUR MOURNERS LASH OUT MINDLESSLY AT EVERYTHING IN SIGHT -- NOTABLY, EACH OTHER.

"YES, I FULLY EXPECT MY LOVELY CHAPEL TO BE THOROUGHLY DEMOLISHED. DON'T WORRY -- INSURANCE WILL COVER IT. THE SPEAKERS ARE FACTORY-TESTED TO BE THE LAST THINGS TO GO.

"WHO DO YOU THINK WILL BE IN ATTENDANCE? CERTAINLY ALL OF THE AVENGERS, PERHAPS THE FANTASTIC FOUR, SPIDER-MAN--?

"THEN FROM MY BUNKER BENEATH THE CHAPEL, I WILL ACTIVATE MY UNDERTAKER MACHINE, SENDING A SUBLIMINAL MESSAGE INTO THE BRAINS OF ALL THOSE IN ATTENDANCE IN THE FORM OF SHMALTZY ORGAN MUSIC--

"--PIPED THROUGH THE NUMEROUS HIDDEN SPEAKERS IN THE CHAPEL.

"THE MUSIC CONTAINS SPECIAL SONIC FREQUENCIES DEVISED TO DIRECTLY STIMULATE THE RAGE CENTERS OF LIVING BRAINS.

"IN THE AFTERMATH, THERE WILL PROBABLY BE A FEW SURVIVORS...THE MIGHTIEST OF YOUR NUMBER.

"EVEN IF THEY FIND EVIDENCE OF MENTAL MANIPULATION, WHICH I DOUBT, THEY WILL NEVER BE ABLE TO FORGIVE THEMSELVES FOR THE SLAUGHTER OF THEIR COMRADES.

"THE RANKS OF YOU SUPER-TYPES WILL HAVE BEEN SEVERELY THINNED. THE CONFIDENCE OF THE SURVIVORS WILL BE SERIOUSLY UNDERMINED. WHY, I WOULD NOT DOUBT IF THE GOVERNMENT WILL BEGIN TO MAKE A MAJOR EFFORT TO CURTAIL THE ACTIVITIES OF YOU COSTUMED VIGILANTES.

'BRILLIANTLY DEVIOUS, EH?'

NICE BEDTIME STORY, BUT I'M NOT SLEEPY. JUST ONE QUESTION, CROSSY-- HOW COME I GET THE HONOR OF BEING THE BAIT FOR YOUR TRAP?

I WOULD THINK IT WAS OBVIOUS, HAWKEYE. YOU ARE THE WEAKEST, MOST VULNERABLE KNOWN COSTUMED CRIMEFIGHTER IN TOWN.

THE...WEAKEST, HUH? WELL, IF I'M SO WEAK, WHY HAVEN'T YOU ACED ME ALREADY?

ALL IN GOOD TIME, ARCHER. BEFORE I HAVE YOU KILLED, I HAVE ONE PRIOR USE FOR YOU.

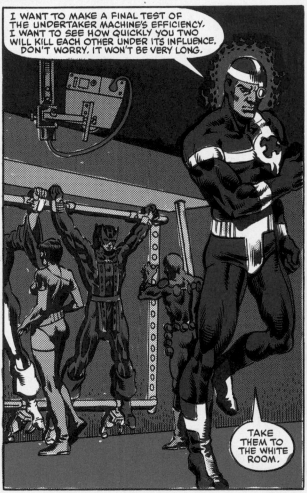

I WANT TO MAKE A FINAL TEST OF THE UNDERTAKER MACHINE'S EFFICIENCY. I WANT TO SEE HOW QUICKLY YOU TWO WILL KILL EACH OTHER UNDER ITS INFLUENCE. DON'T WORRY. IT WON'T BE VERY LONG.

TAKE THEM TO THE WHITE ROOM.

AW, YOU GUYS ARE NO FUN. YOU CAN'T EVEN STAND UP. MAYBE BECAUSE I ADJUSTED YOUR RESTRAINTS PERSONALLY TO AFFORD YOU MAXIMUM DISCOMFORT, HUH?

LEGS AND ARMS NUMB.

NOW WE'RE GONNA HAVE TO LUG YOU ALL THE WAY. PARDON ME FOR SAYING SO, BUT YOU TWO ARE A REAL DRAG.

KEEP BLABBIN', BALLZO! YOU'RE GONNA GET YOURS.

SAY, BOMBSHELL, I DO BELIEVE I'VE BEEN THREATENED.

AH...GOOD TO SEE YOU BACK ON YOUR FEET AGAIN. THIS WOULD BE A LOT LESS INTERESTING IF YOU TWO WERE FLAILING ABOUT ON THE FLOOR. THERE ARE JUST A FEW THINGS I'D LIKE YOU TO KNOW BEFORE THE TEST BEGINS.

FIRST, AS IS OBVIOUS, YOU HAVE BOTH BEEN STRIPPED OF YOUR WEAPONS. YOUR FINAL MINUTES ON EARTH WILL BE SPENT EXERCISING YOUR UNARMED COMBAT SKILLS ONLY.

SECOND, THE ULTRA-SOUND SPEAKERS OF THE UNDERTAKER MACHINERY ARE WELL PROTECTED AGAINST ACCIDENTAL OR INTENTIONAL DAMAGE. I DOUBT YOU'LL EVEN BE ABLE TO DETERMINE WHERE IT IS.

AND FINALLY, CONSIDERING YOUR TRAINING AND BACKGROUNDS, MY BET IS THAT HAWKEYE WILL DIE FIRST. THAT IS ALL.

WISE GUY.

NOT SO MUCH AS A CRACK IN THE WHOLE PLACE. THE DOOR'S AS TIGHT AS A BANK VAULT'S.

CAN'T FIND ANY CAMOUFLAGE PANELS WHERE THE SPEAKERS MIGHT BE. THEY'RE PROBABLY ON THE CEILING OUT OF REACH.

UH, MOCK? COME HERE.

SURE, HAWKEYE.

LISTEN, THERE'S THREE CAMERAS ON US AND THEY'RE PROBABLY RIGGED TO PICK UP SOUND. IF WE HAVE ANY PLANS TO MAKE, WE'D BETTER WHISPER AND KEEP OUR BACKS TO THE CAMERAS.

SURE. YOU HAVE A PLAN?

NOT REALLY. YOU?

NOPE, EXCEPT TRY TO RESIST THE ULTRASOUND BRAINWASHING. SHIELD DID TRAIN ME IN CERTAIN TECHNIQUES.

I'LL DO MY BEST TO RESIST, TOO. I REALLY DON'T WANT TO HURT YOU. IN THE LAST COUPLE DAYS, I'VE ACTUALLY KIND OF STARTED, WELL, LIKING YOU.

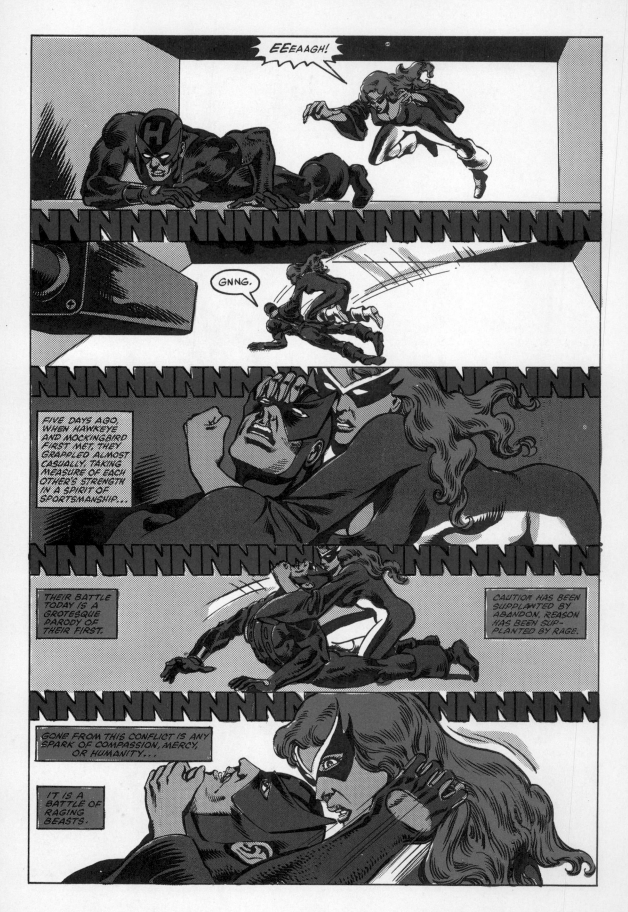

SAY, CROSSFIRE, I'VE BEEN WONDERING... HOW LONG AFTER YOU TURN THE SOUND MACHINE OFF DOES ITS EFFECTS LAST? HOW LONG FOR THEIR BRAINS TO RETURN TO NORMAL?

INTERESTING QUESTION! PERHAPS A BRIEF REVERSION TO NORMAL WILL MAKE THEIR PLIGHT ALL THE MORE POIGNANT. LET US SEE.

NNNNNNNNNNE

OH! STOPPED JUST IN TIME.

I FEEL SO SICK. I-I TRIED TO KILL YOU, HAWKEYE!

FORGET IT, KID. WHAT DO YOU THINK I WAS DOING?

GOTTA THINK. CROSS WOULDN'T HAVE STOPPED HIS TEST FOR NO REASON. HE'S PLANNING SOMETHING.

THERE'S GOT TO BE SOMETHING I CAN DO TO JAM THAT ULTRA-SOUND. MAYBE--!

NOW TO SLOWLY, CASUALLY REMOVE ONE OF HIS HARD-BALLS FROM HIS BELT--

--AND--

DNNK!

ODDBALL-- WHAT'S--

OH, PLEASE LET ME MAKE THIS ONE SHOT. PLEASE!!!

OH--!

I DID IT!

DON'T KNOW HOW LONG THEY'LL BE OUT. NO TIME TO CHECK. I'VE GOT TO GET TO CROSSFIRE BEFORE HE CATCHES ON TO WHAT'S HAPPENING.

MOCKINGBIRD, PLEASE BE OKAY UNTIL I GET BACK. I SWEAR I'LL MAKE ALL THIS UP TO YOU!

CONCUSSIVE ARROW GOING OFF AT HIS FEET!

WEAKEST HERO IN TOWN, AM I, SUCKER? THEN WHAT DOES THAT MAKE YOU? YOU DIDN'T HAVE THE STRENGTH TO PULL MY 250 POUND BOW!

AAH, HE'S OUT OF IT. I'LL BIND HIM UP WITH SOME CORD IN MY QUIVER.

MAN-- AM I EVER GLAD TO HAVE THESE BABIES BACK IN MY HAND. I FEEL LIKE I CAN LICK THE WORLD NOW!

AND, AFTER SECURING CROSSFIRE...

I ALMOST HOPE ODDBALL AND BOMBSHELL HAVE COME TO THEIR SENSES, I'D LIKE TO SHOOT THEM SO FULL OF ARROWS THEY LOOK LIKE OVERSIZED PINCUSHIONS.

IF THESE JOKERS HAVE MADE ME KILL MOCKING-BIRD, I SWEAR THERE'S GONNA BE FOUR COFFINS PUT TO USE IN THIS JOINT.

NO MOVEMENT. THEY'RE ALL STILL OUT.

MOCKINGBIRD--?

ABOUT AN HOUR LATER...

RECEIVING

Restwell Funeral Parlour

YEAH, OFFICER, IT WAS A TOUGH ONE ALL RIGHT, I'LL BE OKAY, REALLY.

SURE YOU DON'T WANT US TO CALL AN AMBULANCE?

PO ICE

NAH. WE'LL DROP BY THE PRECINCT TOMORROW TO PRESS CHARGES, OKAY? WATCH OUT FOR THEM, THEY'RE REAL SNAKES.

OH OH, SHE'S TAKEN CARE OF BUSINESS AND COMING THIS WAY. I-I CAN'T LET HER KNOW THAT I THINK I'VE GONE DEAF, I COULDN'T STOMACH PITY.

WELL, GOOD LOOKING, WE MADE IT. YOU REALLY ARE SOMETHING. I STILL DON'T KNOW HOW YOU GOT US OUT OF THAT PLACE IN AS FEW PIECES AS YOU DID.

MMM-HMMM.

LOOK, I'M NOT MUCH OF A JOINER OR ANYTHING, BUT I MUST ADMIT THAT THE TWO OF US MADE ONE HECKUVA TEAM. I WAS THINKING...MAYBE WE OUGHT TO BECOME AN ITEM, YOU KNOW WHAT I MEAN?

AFTER ALL, YOU ARE ONE OF THE CUTEST--

YEAH, WELL, SEE YOU AROUND THEN.

WHAAAAT? WHAT'S WITH HIM? I WAS PRACTICALLY PROPOSING TO HIM AND HE JUST TURNS AROUND AND WALKS OFF, WHO THE THE HECK DOES HE THINK HE IS, THE CREEP?

I HAVEN'T THE SLIGHTEST IDEA WHAT SHE WAS SAYING, BUT IF I STICK AROUND FOR EVEN ANOTHER SECOND, I KNOW SHE'LL FIND OUT WHAT HAPPENED TO ME.

PROBABLY WASN'T SAYING ANYTHING IMPORTANT ANYWAY.

94

EPILOG

ONE WEEK LATER, THE POCONO MOUNTAINS, NEW YORK...

YOU'RE REALLY IMPOSSIBLE, YOU KNOW THAT?

YOUR STUPID MASCULINE PRIDE NEARLY WRECKED THE GREATEST RELATIONSHIP THIS BLASTED PLANET IS EVER GOING TO SEE BEFORE IT HAD A CHANCE TO GET GOING.

IF I HADN'T RUN AFTER YOU AND FORCED YOU TO EXPLAIN TO ME THE REASON FOR YOUR ASININE BEHAVIOR, WE WOULDN'T BE HERE TODAY.

DO NOT DIS-TURB

YOU OWE ME, PAL. SURE, YOU SAVED MY LIFE. BUT WHAT I'M GOING TO DO TO YOUR LIFE IS MORE THAN JUST A ONE-SHOT DEAL.

I'M NOT JUST TALKING ABOUT HELPING YOU GET A HEARING AID, OR THE BLOOD TEST, OR THE LICENSE, OR EVEN ARRANGING FOR A QUAINT LITTLE COTTAGE IN THE WOODS.

I'M TALKING ABOUT THE REST OF YOUR LIFE, AND THE DIFFERENCE HAVING ME AROUND IS GOING TO MAKE IN IT. MAYBE ELOPING WAS MY IDEA, BUT I'M GOING TO SEE TO IT THAT FOR THE REST OF YOUR LIFE, YOU BELIEVE THAT IT WAS THE BEST IDEA YOU DIDN'T QUITE HEAR.

I HEAR YOU, MRS. HAWKEYE. I HEAR YOU.

The Beginning...